The Sleeping Beauty

Retold by Annette Smith
Illustrated by Margaret Power

Once upon a time, there lived a king and a queen in a faraway kingdom. For many years they had no children. Then, to their joy, the queen gave birth to a little girl. She was so beautiful that the queen named her Briar Rose.

The king gave a great feast for the baby's naming ceremony. He invited all the lords and ladies in the land. As special guests, the king and queen invited four fairies to be godmothers to the little princess.

Everyone was very happy as they gathered around the cradle in the great hall.

After the feast, each fairy godmother presented the princess with a special gift. One gave her the gift of joy, and another the gift of kindness, and another the gift of wisdom.

Just as the youngest fairy was waving her wand over the cradle, the door to the great hall was flung open and in came a wicked fairy. She was dressed in black, and she shrieked loudly at the king, "Why didn't you invite me?"

Because she had been left out, the wicked fairy was very jealous. "I will get even with you all," she said, glaring at the king and queen. She leaned over the cradle and screamed, "The princess will prick her finger on a spinning wheel and die!"

Everyone gasped in horror.

All the guests fell silent as the wicked fairy stormed out of the great hall.

Then the youngest fairy stepped forward. "I have not made my wish yet," she said. "I cannot undo the wish of another fairy, but I can change it a little. This is my wish for the little princess: if she pricks her finger on a spinning wheel she will not die. She will sleep for a hundred years, instead."

The king immediately ordered all spinning wheels in the castle to be burned. The little princess grew up without knowing what a spinning wheel was.

As the years went by, every wish that the good fairies made came true. Briar Rose grew wiser and more joyful every day, and she was always kind and loving. Rosebushes as beautiful as the young princess bloomed around the castle. The king and queen hardly ever thought about the wicked fairy's wish.

Just before Briar Rose turned sixteen, a splendid party was planned for her birthday.

On her sixteenth birthday, Briar Rose was so excited that she couldn't stay in her rooms, just waiting for the celebrations to begin. She felt she had to do something. So she ran along the castle passages and up some winding stairs. She came to a little room at the top of a narrow turret.

"I have never been here before," she said, turning the rusty key in the lock. Briar Rose opened the door and went inside. To her surprise, she saw an old woman sitting at a strange-looking object with a wheel that whirred around and around.

"Come in, my dear. Come in," said the old woman, beckoning to her.

"What are you doing?" asked Briar Rose.

"I am spinning," replied the old woman. "Come over here and try it."

As Briar Rose reached out to touch the spinning wheel, she pricked her finger on the spindle and she fell to the ground.

The old woman, who was really the wicked fairy in disguise, gave a nasty laugh and disappeared out the window.

In the meantime, the celebrations were about to begin, and the king and queen and all the ladies-in-waiting were searching the castle for Briar Rose.

At last the king, to his horror, found her slumped on the floor beside the spinning wheel in the little room at the top of the winding stairs. He knew that the wicked fairy had carried out her curse.

The king carried Briar Rose down to her own rooms, where her ladies-in-waiting dressed her in her finest gown.

The youngest fairy returned to the castle at once. She knew that all she could do was make sure everything would be unchanged when the beautiful princess awoke from her long sleep.

The fairy waved her magic wand and everyone fell asleep — the king and queen, the lords and ladies, the servants, and the cook. Every living creature inside the castle walls fell asleep – the horses in their stables, the dogs in their kennels, and the mice in their holes. Then the youngest fairy disappeared, leaving the castle to slumber for a hundred years.

All was quiet and still.

As the years went by, the trees and bushes grew higher and thicker around the castle walls, until the castle was hidden from sight. But the beautiful briar roses in the castle gardens bloomed inside the castle walls.

A hundred years later, a handsome young prince heard about the legend of the sleeping princess. Many princes before him had tried to cut down the tangled growth that surrounded the castle, but they had all failed. They found that they could not cut down a single vine.

But the handsome young prince was determined to succeed. He found the thicket that surrounded the castle and began to slash at the plants. The bushes and brambles and wild roses parted and made a passage for him to ride through. Then, as if by magic, the castle door swung open with a loud creak.

The prince stepped over sleeping servants, past lords and ladies slumped in their chairs, and walked along the dusty passages. Finally he came to the room where Briar Rose had been sleeping for a hundred years.

The prince was overwhelmed when he saw the beautiful young princess. He went over to the bed and knelt beside her. As he took her hand, she opened her eyes and looked at him.

At once, everything in the castle began to stir. The king and queen, the lords and ladies, and the servants woke up and yawned and stretched. The cook stoked the fire and went on preparing the food for the feast, as though she had never been asleep. Outside, in the castle grounds, the birds began to sing, dogs could be heard barking, and the horses moved restlessly in their stables.

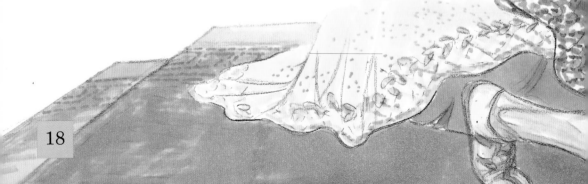

The wicked fairy's spell was over at last.

The handsome prince married Briar Rose, the Sleeping Beauty, and together they brought great happiness to all who lived in the kingdom.

A play
The Sleeping Beauty

People in the play

Narrator	Prince
Briar Rose	Wicked fairy (Old woman)
King	Youngest fairy
Queen	Lords and ladies (walk-on roles)

 Three fairies

Scene One — In a castle

Narrator

Once upon a time, there lived a king and a queen in a faraway kingdom. For many years they had no children. Then, to their joy, the queen gave birth to a little girl.

Queen

Our little daughter is so beautiful. She has the delicate features of a rose. We shall call her Briar Rose.

King

We will give a great feast in her honor. It will be her naming ceremony. We will invite all the lords and ladies in the land. As special guests, we must invite four good fairies to be our little daughter's godmothers.

Narrator

The naming ceremony was a wonderful occasion. Everyone was very happy as they gathered around the cradle.

First fairy

Now that the feast is over, it is time for us to present the little princess with our special gifts. I give this beautiful child the gift of joy.

Second fairy

I give the little princess the gift of kindness.

Third fairy

My gift to Briar Rose is the gift of wisdom.

Narrator

Just as the youngest fairy was waving her wand over the cradle, the door to the great hall was flung open. In came a wicked fairy.

Wicked fairy (shrieking loudly)

Why didn't you invite me? Why was I left out? I will get even with you all. The princess will prick her finger on a spinning wheel and die!

Narrator

Everyone gasped in horror as the wicked fairy stormed out of the great hall.

Youngest fairy (stepping forward)

I have not made my wish yet. I cannot undo the wish of another fairy, but I can change it a little. This is my wish for the little princess: if she pricks her finger on a spinning wheel she will not die. She will sleep for a hundred years, instead.

King

This cannot happen to my daughter. I order that all the spinning wheels in this castle be burned.

Narrator

The little princess grew up without knowing what a spinning wheel was. As the years went by, every wish that the good fairies made came true. Briar Rose grew wiser and more joyful every day. She was always kind and loving. Rosebushes as beautiful as the young princess bloomed around the castle. The king and queen hardly ever thought about the wicked fairy's wish.

Scene Two — The castle, sixteen years later

King

Briar Rose is nearly sixteen years old. We will have a splendid party for her birthday.

Briar Rose (to her ladies-in-waiting)

Today is my birthday. I am so excited about the party that I can't stay here in my rooms. I have to do something.

Narrator

Briar Rose ran along the castle passages and up some winding stairs. She came to a little room at the top of a narrow turret.

Briar Rose

I have never been here before. I will just turn this key and peep inside the room.

Narrator

To her surprise, Briar Rose saw an old woman (who was really the wicked fairy) sitting beside a strange-looking object.

Old woman (Wicked fairy)

Come in, my dear. Come in.

Briar Rose

What are you doing?

Old woman (Wicked fairy)

I am spinning. Come over here and try.

Narrator

As Briar Rose reached out to touch the spinning wheel, she pricked her finger on the spindle and she fell to the ground. The wicked fairy gave a nasty laugh and disappeared out the window. In the meantime, the birthday celebrations were about to begin.

Queen

Where is Briar Rose? We cannot start the celebrations without her. Where can she be?

King

We shall have to go and look for her.

Narrator

The king and queen and all the ladies-in-waiting searched the castle. At last the king, to his horror, found Briar Rose slumped on the floor beside the spinning wheel, in the little room at the top of the winding stairs.

King

Oh, no! The wicked fairy has carried out her curse. I cannot wake Briar Rose. I will carry her down to her rooms and have her ladies-in-waiting dress her in her finest gown. She will sleep for a hundred years.

Narrator

The youngest fairy knew that the wicked fairy had carried out her curse. She came to the castle at once.

Youngest fairy (waving her magic wand)

All I can do is make sure that everything in the castle will be unchanged when the beautiful princess wakes up from her long sleep. Now I will put everyone in this castle to sleep. First the king and the queen, then the lords and ladies, and now the servants and the cook.

Narrator

The youngest fairy put every living creature inside the castle walls to sleep — the horses in their stables, the dogs in their kennels, and the mice in their holes.

Youngest fairy

Now that every living thing is asleep, I will leave the castle to slumber for a hundred years.

Narrator

The youngest fairy disappeared and all was quiet and still. As the years went by, the trees and bushes grew higher and thicker around the castle walls, until the castle was hidden from sight. But the beautiful briar roses in the castle gardens bloomed inside the castle walls.

Scene Three — The castle, a hundred years later

Narrator

A hundred years later, a handsome prince heard about the legend of the sleeping princess.

Prince

Many other princes before me have found the castle where the princess sleeps, but they have not been able to cut down the tangled growth that surrounds the walls. I am determined to succeed where they have failed.

Narrator

At last the prince found the thicket that surrounded the castle, and he began to slash at the plants.

Prince

I cannot believe this. The bushes and brambles and wild roses are parting, making a passage for me to ride through.

Narrator

The castle door swung open with a loud creak.

Prince

The legend is true. Everyone here in this castle is asleep. The cook is asleep. The servants are asleep, and, over there, the lords and ladies are asleep, too.

Narrator

The prince walked along the dusty passages until he came to the room where Briar Rose had been sleeping for a hundred years.

Prince

The princess is so beautiful.

Narrator

The prince went over to the bed and knelt beside her. As he took her hand, she opened her eyes and looked at him.

Prince

I want to marry you, Briar Rose.

Narrator

At once, everything in the castle began to stir. The king and queen, the lords and ladies, and the servants woke up and yawned and stretched. The cook stoked the fire and went on preparing food for the feast, as though she had never been asleep. Outside, in the castle grounds, the birds began to sing, dogs could be heard barking, and the horses moved restlessly in their stables.

Prince

The wicked fairy's spell is over.

Narrator

The handsome prince married Briar Rose, the Sleeping Beauty, and together they brought great happiness to all who lived in the kingdom.